The European Union

Political, Social, and Economic Cooperation

GERMANY

by
Ida Walker

Mason Crest Publishers
Philadelphia

Mason Crest Publishers Inc.
370 Reed Road, Broomall, Pennsylvania 19008
(866) MCP-BOOK (toll free)
www.masoncrest.com

First printing
1 2 3 4 5 6 7 8 9 10

Library of Congress Cataloging-in-Publication Data

Walker, Ida.
  Germany / by Ida Walker.
     p. cm.—(The European Union / Ida Walker)
  Includes bibliographical references and index.
   ISBN 1-4222-0048-5
   ISBN 1-4222-0038-8 (series)
1. Germany—History—Juvenile literature. 2. Germany—Description and travel—Juvenile literature. 3. Germany—Social life and customs—Juvenile literature. 4. European Union—Germany—Juvenile literature. I. Title.
   DD17.W35 2006
   943—dc22
                          2005004075

Produced by Harding House Publishing Service, Inc.
www.hardinghousepages.com
Interior design by Benjamin Stewart
Cover design by MK Bassett-Harvey.
Printed in the Hashemite Kingdom of Jordan.

CONTENTS

THE
EUROPEAN
UNION

GREENLAND
SEA

BARENTS
SEA

★ Reykjavik ICELAND

NORWEGIAN
SEA

White
Sea

FINLAND

Tampere ●

NORWAY

RUSSIA

Gulf of
Bothnia

Turku ● Helsinki ✪

★ Moscow

Oslo ✪

Stockholm ✪

Tallinn ★

ESTONIA

Tartu ●

SWEDEN

Gulf of
Riga

LATVIA

Gothenburg ●

Riga ★

Helsingborg ●

BALTIC
SEA

LITHUANIA

UNITED KINGDOM

DENMARK

Kaunas ●
Vilnius ★

IRELAND

NORTH SEA

Copenhagen ✪

Dublin ✪

RUSSIA

★ Minsk

Gdansk ●

THE NETHERLANDS

Hamburg ●

BELARUS

London ✪

Amsterdam ✪

Berlin ✪

POLAND

Warsaw ✪

BELGIUM

Brussels ✪

GERMANY

Leipzig ●

Wroclaw ●

LUXEMBOURG

Luxembourg ★

Prague ✪

UKRAINE

Paris ✪

CZECH REPUBLIC

Krakow ●

★ Kyiv

Stuttgart ●

SLOVAKIA

Munich ●

Vienna ✪

Bratislava ★

MOLDOVA

FRANCE

SWITZERLAND

Bern ★

AUSTRIA

HUNGARY

Budapest ✪

Sea of
Azov

ROMANIA

Ljubljana ✪

SLOVENIA

★ Bucharest

BLACK
SEA

ITALY

Zagreb ★

BOSNIA-
HERCEGOVINA
CROATIA

Belgrade ★

YUGOSLAVIA

BULGARIA

Rome ●

Sofia ★

MACEDONIA

★ Ankara

TURKEY

ALBANIA

Thessaloniki ●

PORTUGAL

Madrid ★

Lisbon ●

SPAIN

GREECE

Seville ●

Athens ●

MEDITERRANEAN SEA

IONIAN
SEA

TYRRHENIAN
SEA

AEGEAN
SEA

Sea of Crete

Lefkosia
(Nicosia) ✪

CYPRUS

SYRIA

LEBANON

MOROCCO

★ Rabat

ALGERIA

MALTA

✪ Valetta

MEDITERRANEAN SEA

JORD

Strait of Gibraltar

TUNISIA

ISRAEL &
THE PALESTINIAN
TERRITORIES

LIBYA

GERMANY
European Union Member since 1952

Flensburg
Puttgarden
Sassnitz
Kiel
Stralsund
Rostock
Schwenn
Hamburg
Wilhelmshaven
Bremerhaven
Emden
Oldenburg
Bremen
Wittenberge
★ Berlin
Potsdam
Osanbruck
Hannover
Braunschweig
Magdeburg
Bielefeld
Münster
Dessau
Cottbus
Duisburg
Dortmund
Göttingen
Halle
Essen
Leipzig
Dusseldorf
Willingen
Kassel
Görlitz
Dresden
Cologne
Erfurt
Aachen
Siegen
Weimar
Chemnitz
Bonn
Bad
Hersfeld
Jena
Zwickau
Gera
Hof
Weisbaden
Frankfurt
Bamberg
Mainz
Würzburg
Mannheim
Nürnberg
Heidelberg
Saarbrücken
Heilbronn
Regensburg
Karlsruhe
Passau
Stuttgart
Ulm
Augsburg
Munich
Freiburg
Konstanz

INTRODUCTION

Sixty years ago, Europe lay scarred from the battles of the Second World War. During the next several years, a plan began to take shape that would unite the countries of the European continent so that future wars would be inconceivable. On May 9, 1950, French Foreign Minister Robert Schuman issued a declaration calling on France, Germany, and other European countries to pool together their coal and steel production as "the first concrete foundation of a European federation." "Europe Day" is celebrated each year on May 9 to commemorate the beginning of the European Union (EU).

The EU consists of twenty-five countries, spanning the continent from Ireland in the west to the border of Russia in the east. Eight of the ten most recently admitted EU member states are former communist regimes that were behind the Iron Curtain for most of the latter half of the twentieth century.

Any European country with a democratic government, a functioning market economy, respect for fundamental rights, and a government capable of implementing EU laws and policies may apply for membership. Bulgaria and Romania are set to join the EU in 2007. Croatia and Turkey have also embarked on the road to EU membership.

While the EU began as an idea to ensure peace in Europe through interconnected economies, it has evolved into so much more today:

- Citizens can travel freely throughout most of the EU without carrying a passport and without stopping for border checks.

- EU citizens can live, work, study, and retire in another EU country if they wish.

- The euro, the single currency accepted throughout twelve of the EU countries (with more to come), is one of the EU's most tangible achievements, facilitating commerce and making possible a single financial market that benefits both individuals and businesses.

- The EU ensures cooperation in the fight against cross-border crime and terrorism.

- The EU is spearheading world efforts to preserve the environment.

- As the world's largest trading bloc, the EU uses its influence to promote fair rules for world trade, ensuring that globalization also benefits the poorest countries.

- The EU is already the world's largest donor of humanitarian aid and development assistance, providing 55 percent of global official development assistance to developing countries in 2004.

The EU is neither a nation intended to replace existing nations, nor an international organization. The EU is unique—its member countries have established common institutions to which they delegate some of their sovereignty so that decisions on matters of joint interest can be made democratically at the European level.

Europe is a continent with many different traditions and languages, but with shared values such as democracy, freedom, and social justice, cherished values well known to North Americans. Indeed, the EU motto is "United in Diversity."

Enjoy your reading. Take advantage of this chance to learn more about Europe and the EU!

Ambassador John Bruton,
Head of Delegation of the European Commission, Washington, D.C.

Organic farming has deep roots in Germany.

THE LANDSCAPE

Guten Tag! Welcome to Germany, "the **Pivot** of Europe." Situated right in the heart of Europe, Germany has historically functioned as a crossroads for many peoples, ideas, and even armies. Now it provides a natural gateway connecting its traditional Western European trading partners to the fast-growing Central and East European economies.

Germany is the seventh-largest country in Europe. About the size of the state of Montana, it covers an area of 137,847 square miles (357,021 sq. kilometers). Nine nations and two seas form Germany's borders. The North Sea, Denmark, and the Baltic Sea lie to the north. Poland and Czech Republic border Germany on the east. The countries of Austria and Switzerland form the southern border, and France, Belgium, the Netherlands, and Luxembourg line Germany's western border. Several islands in the North and Baltic Seas are also included in Germany's territory.

PLAINS, MOUNTAINS, VALLEYS, AND FORESTS

Germany is not a large country. Nevertheless, it boasts a landscape of remarkable diversity. Stretching from coastal plains to mountain ranges, Germany can be divided into three major natural land regions—lowlands in the north, uplands in the center, and mountains in the south.

The North German Plain is a low, flatland mass that lies along and between the North and Baltic Seas, extending southward into eastern Germany. Marshlands, dunes, **fords**, and tidal flats—nearly flat coastal areas, alternately covered and exposed by the tides—mark the German coast.

Wide river valleys cut through the North German Plain, providing soft, fertile land for cultivation. The farmland of the plain's eastern end is so fertile it has been dubbed Germany's bread-basket. Large ports and industrial centers have also developed along the riverbanks. Between the river valleys lie the heathlands—large areas covered with sand and gravel deposited by ancient glaciers. Heather, a low-growing shrub, flourishes in the heathlands' thin soil.

South of the North German Plain are the highlands of central Germany. These uplands are a striking terrain of low mountains, narrow valleys, and small basins. The highest points in central Germany are the Harz Mountains and the Thuringian Forest. Many rivers flow through the region, cutting rugged gorges from its hills. Grapes grow along the rivers' hillsides. At some places, the narrow river valleys widen into small basins that provide excellent farmland. The rivers are **navigable**, which has led to intensive industrial development in the region.

Germany's southern region includes the South German Hills, the Black Forest, and the Bavarian Alps. The region's earlier settlers were engaged primarily in agriculture and tourism. However, since the 1970s, industry has also developed here.

Long parallel ridges called escarpments cross the South German Hills' landscape. Sheep are raised on these rocky ridges. The lowlands

Southern Germany's landscapes are banded with mountains, forests, and farmlands.

between the ridges contain some of Germany's best farmland.

In the southwest corner of Germany is the well-known Black Forest. This mountainous region, the scene of many old German legends and fairy tales, derives its name from the dark fir and spruce trees. Small villages nestle in the forest. The region is famous for its delicious foods, especially its ham and chocolate-cherry cake.

In Germany's southeast corner, on its border with Austria, is Bavaria. This is where the alpine mountains begin. The highest point in Germany,

Quick Facts: The Geography of Germany

Location: Central Europe, bordering the North and Baltic Seas, between the Netherlands and Poland, south of Denmark

Area: Slightly smaller than Montana
>   ***total:*** 137,847 square miles (357,021 sq. km.)
>   ***land:*** 134,836 square miles (349,223 sq. km.)
>   ***water:*** 3,011 square miles (7,798 sq. km.)

Borders: Austria 487 miles (784 km.), Belgium 104 miles (167 km.), Czech Republic 401 miles (646 km.), Denmark 42 miles (68 km.), France 280 miles (451 km.), Luxembourg 86 miles (138 km.), Netherlands 358 miles (577 km.), Poland 283 miles (456 km.), Switzerland 207 miles (334 km.)

Climate: Temperate; cool, cloudy, wet winters and summers; more extreme temperatures inland; south, a colder region

Terrain: Lowlands in north, uplands in center, mountains in south

Elevation Extremes
>   ***Lowest point:*** Neuendorf bei Wilster –11.6 feet (–3.54 meters)
>   ***Highest point:*** Zugspitze 9,719 feet (2,963 meters)

Natural Hazards: Flooding

the 9,719-foot (2,963-meter) peak Zugspitze, is located here. The Bavarian Alps offer fantastic skiing, snowboarding, and sledding.

Rivers and Lakes

Germany claims more than 4,316 miles (6,950 kilometers) of interconnected rivers, canals, and lakes. Over the centuries, great cities have developed along these water routes.

The most important river is the Rhine. Both a tourist river and a busy transport waterway, it forms part of the borders with Switzerland and France before flowing into the Netherlands. The Elbe is another river crucial to German industry and agriculture. The Danube, Main, Neckar, Em, Older, and Weser are other important rivers.

Germany is dotted with **picturesque** lakes. The largest lake is Bondensee, which lies partly in Austria and Switzerland. The glaciers that shaped the land in the last ice age have left behind several small lakes as well.

A Temperate Climate

Germany has a cool, **temperate** climate with abundant rainfall and a long, overcast season. Because of their **proximity** to the sea, the northern lowlands enjoy an especially mild climate. The temperature in the north rarely dips below 30°F (–1°C) in the winter and averages about 64°F (18°C) during the summer.

Temperature ranges increase somewhat in central and southern Germany's uplands. The warmest summer temperatures are in the Rhine Valley and the coldest winter temperatures are in the Alps of the far south. The south also receives the heaviest precipitation, about seventy-eight inches (198 cen-

In the 1790s, Germany's King Wilhelm II gave his girlfriend an artificial "ruin" on Peacock Island in the Havel River in Wannsee, Germany. Today the island is a landscaped garden that tourists visit by ferry.

Lake Hintersee in Bavaria, Germany.

timeters) per year, much of it in the form of snow. The central uplands get about twenty inches (51 centimeters) of precipitation per year, and the lowlands in the north receive about twenty-eight inches (71 centimeters) per year.

TREES, PLANTS, AND WILDLIFE

About one-fourth of Germany is covered with woodlands. Most of the forests are in the south. While nearly a third of the forest cover is mixed, **deciduous** woodland, two-thirds are composed of pine, fir, larch, and other **conifers** growing on higher altitudes. Beech, oak, and walnut trees are the main types of trees found in the lower woodlands. The Alpine region bursts with wildflowers. Berries and mushrooms also grow in abundance.

Germany's wildlife includes deer, wild boars, hares, weasels, badgers, wolves, and foxes. The adder is a poisonous snake found here. Finches, geese, and other **migratory** birds cross the country. Herring, cod, flounder, and ocean perch inhabit the coastal waters. The Alps are home to the snow hare, the alpine marmot, and the golden eagle.

The country is also home to endangered species such as the Eurasian otter, white whale, and lynx. Germany maintains ninety nature parks, thirteen **biosphere** reserves, and thirteen national parks.

A medieval castle overlooks a modern village on the Rhine.

2 GERMANY'S HISTORY AND GOVERNMENT

Germany has not always existed as the country it is today. For centuries, the area was more of a cultural region than a nation. It was comprised of many territories, each fairly independent and ruled by its own leader. The people of these territories were culturally similar, but they were not united under one government. In 1871, these territories came together under a single government, and Germany the **nation-state** was born.

The borders of this first German nation-state, however, are not Germany's borders today. Within a century, the infant nation acquired a dark history: two world wars, a famous dictator and his terrible crimes, several rebellions, and a division of the country. Today, the Federal Republic of Germany stands as a united, democratic country, a leading member of the United Nations, and a central figure in the European Union (EU). As a nation, Germany is committed to peace and shares good relations with other countries. Germany, however, traveled a long road to reach its current state.

ANCIENT GERMANY

Ancient artifacts discovered on German lands indicate the area was home to early human beings 400,000 years ago. The **Celts**, however, were the first recorded people of the territory. Around 1000 BCE, North European tribes began migrating to the area. By 100 BCE, they had conquered the Celts and taken over the land completely.

The Romans dubbed these tribes Germani, and the land became known as Germania. The Germanic tribes were mostly farmers and hunters. The Romans called them barbarians and tried to push the Germani back, but after losing a major battle in 9 CE, the Romans started instead building barriers to keep out the Germanic tribes. Slowly, the Roman Empire collapsed, and then it was the tribes' turn to plunder Rome. The western portion of the Roman Empire came under Germanic control in the 400s and was carved into tribal kingdoms.

The Franks emerged as the most powerful tribe in the region. Charlemagne, a Frank and the greatest ruler of the era, built an empire that extended over Germany, France, and much of central Italy. Civil wars followed Charlemagne's death, and his sons divided their father's empire into three kingdoms.

THE HOLY ROMAN EMPIRE

Eventually, the Frank dynasty died out in Germany and gave way to the Saxons. Otto I, a strong Saxon emperor, founded the Holy Roman Empire in 962 CE. The Holy Roman Empire, not to be confused with the Roman Empire (31 BCE–476 CE), is often called the First German Reich, that is, German Empire. However, it was neither fully German nor a proper empire.

The Holy Roman Empire was a group of Western and Central European territories that stood united by Christianity. While there was one supreme emperor, each territory had its own individual ruler. Constant struggles between these rulers and the empire marked the period. The crown and the Roman Catholic Church were also locked in a power struggle.

In the early stages of the empire, the emperors were very powerful. But as time passed, they were forced to grant more and more power to territorial rulers. The **feudal system** became stronger. The **nobility**, a new class that challenged the emperor, emerged.

A fourteenth-century painting of Charlemagne. Today the painting is in Karlstein Castle.

DATING SYSTEMS AND THEIR MEANING

You might be accustomed to seeing dates expressed with the abbreviations BC or AD, as in the year 1000 BC or the year AD 1900. For centuries, this dating system has been the most common in the Western world. However, since BC and AD are based on Christianity (BC stands for Before Christ and AD stands for *anno Domini*, Latin for "in the year of our Lord"), many people now prefer to use abbreviations that people from all religions can be comfortable using. The abbreviations BCE (meaning Before Common Era) and CE (meaning Common Era, mark time in the same way (for example, 1000 BC is the same year as 1000 BCE, and AD 1900 is the same year as 1900 CE), but BCE and CE do not have the same religious overtones as BC and AD.

At its peak, the empire contained most of the territory that makes up today's Germany, Austria, Slovenia, Switzerland, Belgium, the Netherlands, Luxembourg, the Czech Republic, eastern France, northern Italy, and western Poland. Later, many regions broke away. Though the Holy Roman Emperors continued to rule the German territories (and to some extent Italy) until 1806, the empire was reduced to a collection of more-or-less independent states and cities.

THE REFORMATION

The sixteenth century brought a new age to Europe: the Reformation. People started questioning the practices of the Roman Catholic Church. This led to the creation of a new Christian group, the Protestants, or those who protest.

The movement influenced the German territories too. In 1517, Martin Luther, a German monk, led a revolt against the Church. Lutheranism, the Protestant group founded by Luther, quickly gained a following throughout the country.

The Reformation sparked an era of unrest in the German territories. German peasants, who lived under miserable conditions, revolted against the lords. Although the peasants' demands were economic and not religious, the Reformation provoked them into launching a full-scale revolt. The rebellion led to the Peasants' War (1524–1526), but the peasants were brutally crushed.

The Protestant movement also led to other religious and political divisions, and wars broke out throughout the empire. By 1555, a settlement was struck that recognized Lutheranism as the religion of most of the northern and central German territories. Struggles between Catholics and Protestants, however, did not end with the settlement. Tensions eventually erupted into a series of wars collectively known as the Thirty Years War (1618–1648). The Peace of Westphalia ended the conflicts, but the German territories remained overwhelmingly divided.

The German city of Brandenburgertor in 1907.

THE DEUTSCHES REICH

The German territories had to pay a heavy price for their divided state: France launched a series of aggressions and captured large portions of the region. By 1806, the French general Napoleon Bonaparte dissolved Germany's Holy Roman Empire completely.

The defeat awakened a sense of **nationalism** in the German territories. They banded together under the Prussian banner (Prussia was the largest German state) and fought the War of Liberation against the French in 1813. The German territories won, and a loose **confederation** was established.

In 1862, Prussia's prime minister, Otto Von Bismarck, took up the cause of German **unification**. He gathered the German states together to launch successful campaigns against their neighboring states. Encouraged by his success, the German states decided to unite fully. On January 18, 1871, they accepted Prussian King William I as their emperor and announced the establishment of the Deutsches Reich. With this, Germany the nation-state was born.

The Deutsches Reich provided for a democratically elected **parliament**, the Reichstag, but granted it only limited powers. It also gave powers to individual states, though the real authority rested with the Prussian emperor, the kaiser.

WORLD WAR I AND THE WEIMAR REPUBLIC

During the period 1871–1910, the Reich fared well, but then the tide turned and things started to sour. A severe economic depression gripped the land. **Socialism** became a louder voice. The German working class demanded democracy; they wanted the Reichstag to have real powers. Then came World War I, and the situation worsened.

The war started on June 28, 1914, when Gavrilo Princip, a member of the Black Hand, a Serbian **nationalist** group, assassinated Archduke Ferdinand and his wife Sophie of Austria. Russia supported Serbia and Germany supported Austria, so Germany declared war on Russia. After France stepped in on the Russian side, Germany attacked France. Since the quickest route to Paris was through Belgium, German troops invaded that **neutral** country. Great Britain then declared war on Germany.

At first, German workers supported the war; later they changed their minds. By 1918, when it became clear that Germany had lost the war, worker protests exploded into a revolution. The emperor went into exile, and a new German government, the Weimar Republic, was formed. It asked for peace, but that peace came at a heavy cost. Germany lost both land and money, forcing it to reduce the size of its armed forces.

NAZI GERMANY AND WORLD WAR II

The large **reparations** Germany had to make to the war victors placed a great burden on the country. In 1922–1923, the economy collapsed, and the National Socialist German Workers Party, the Nazi Party, attempted a revolution under their leader, Adolf Hitler. The revolution failed. By the late 1920s, the economy seemed to have recovered, and the country again emerged as a cultural and intellectual center.

The worldwide depression of 1929 cut short the good times. The economy was hit badly, and confusio[n] The Nazi Party grew more powerfu[l] members by offering radical solutions [to the coun]try's economic problems and upholdi[ng] values.

Unfortunately, most people who [supported] Hitler had no idea of his real plans. [After] being appointed as the **chancello**[r]

Adolf Hitler, the Nazi dictator

Adolf Hitler became a dictator. Hitler's Germany was unofficially called the Third Reich.

Hitler considered the German people superior to all others, and wanted only people of German origin to live in Germany. In 1935, he started a horrifying, inhuman campaign to rid the land of Jews and others who he felt "polluted" the German population. In the following years, the Nazi Party systematically killed millions of people in what they referred to as the "Final Solution."

Hitler also wanted to rebuild the German military might it had lost in World War I. In 1936, he formed an alliance with Italy and signed an anti-Communist agreement with Japan. These three powers became known as the Axis powers.

Hitler's plans for Germany also included getting more land. In 1938, Germany occupied Austria, and the next year it seized Czechoslovakia. In August 1939, Germany and the Soviet Union formed a nonaggression pact in which both agreed to remain neutral if the other became involved in a war. Secretly, they also agreed to divide Poland and parts of Eastern Europe between them.

On September 1, 1939, Hitler addressed the Reichstag and claimed that Poland had tried to invade Germany. With that, the German military invaded Poland, and the flames of World War II ignited. To defend Poland, Great Britain and France declared war on Germany two days later. Unfortunately, Poland fell to the Germans (who split the country with the Soviets along previously determined lines), who then went on to capture Denmark, Norway, Luxembourg, and Belgium. In May 1940, France too fell into the Germans' hands. The Balkans and Crete were the sites of the next German victories.

In June 1941, Hitler **reneged** on the nonaggression pact and invaded the Soviet Union. At first the German army met with frightening success, but ultimately the invasion turned out to be a mistake. The massive Soviet Union, its harsh climate, and its **scorched-earth policy** simply could not be defeated. Having advanced within 30 miles (48.3 kilometers) of Moscow, the German troops were now pushed back. Meanwhile, after Japan's attack on Pearl Harbor on December 7, 1941, the United States entered the war. By 1944, Germany was losing the war. Hitler committed suicide on April 30,

1945. A week later, May 7, 1945, the country surrendered. Again, war left Germany in ruins. Rebuilding would be long and hard.

THE DIVISION

In July and August, the leaders of Great Britain, the United States, and the Soviet Union decided to rebuild Germany and placed themselves as its governing body. However, the Allies had severe disagreements, and the country was divided into East and West. West Germany, under British and U.S. control, was named the Federal Republic of Germany. Its capital was Bonn. East Germany, under Soviet control, became the German Democratic Republic, and its capital was East Berlin.

West Germany's government was democratic as well as **capitalist**. It encouraged business, and the economy thrived. East Germany, however, did not fare as well. Ruled by dictators, it was **exploited** by the Soviet Union. The Soviets stopped almost all trade, communication, and travel between the East and West. The **Cold War** had begun.

In 1953, strikes and riots broke out in East Germany. Thousands of East Germans fled to West Germany. In August 1961, the Soviets built the Berlin Wall between East and West Berlin to seal off the border. However, protests continued in East Germany.

On November 9, 1989, the East German government, with the approval and encouragement of Mikhael Gorbachev, the reform-minded Soviet

After 1961, Checkpoint Charlie was one of the few places where people could cross from West Berlin into East Berlin.

leader, finally opened its borders. The Berlin Wall was breached. East Germany started moving toward a more democratic government.

THE UNIFIED GERMANY OF TODAY

As democracy took root in East Germany, people began considering a unified Germany. East Germany announced its desire for unification in February 1990. In May of that year, East and West Germany signed a treaty for close economic cooperation, and in July the economies of East and West Germany were united.

On October 3, 1990, the unification of the countries was completed. Since East Germany was not prosperous, the unification placed a heavy economic burden on West Germany. But the country has struggled past the many challenges it faced.

Today's Germany is a federation of sixteen states. It is a multiparty democracy. The country's parliament has two houses: *Bundersat* is the upper house and *Bundestag* the lower house. Together, the two houses elect their president, who in turn appoints the chancellor, with whom the real power rests.

After two world wars and spending decades divided, Germany has come a long way in its political and economic development. It is now a country of strength and central importance in the European Union. It is also Europe's economic powerhouse.

Berlin's Trep Towers, a gleaming modern office complex.

3 THE ECONOMY

Germany is a giant on the world economic stage and overshadows all its European neighbors. Germany has one of the world's most powerful economies, and it is the second-largest importer and exporter. It is also a member of the powerful G7—the seven leading industrial nations in the world.

Berlin is a busy modern city.

A Social Market Economy

Germany's success lies in the social market economy structure that it adopted during World War II. A social market economy has both material (financial) and social (human) dimensions.

The two main aspects of a social market economy are **entrepreneurial** responsibility and competition. It is an entrepreneur's responsibility to see to her company's growth and to ensure that it can adapt to changing circumstances. The government's role is limited to creating conditions favor-

able to a healthy economy by contributing to the **infrastructure**, as well as fair labor and tax laws. The government is also committed to helping those unable to cope with the strenuous demands of a competitive market.

THE NEW ECONOMY

Although one-third of Germany's **gross domestic product** (GDP) comes from its manufacturing giants, the dominant source of Germany's income today comes from the service sector, which contributes two-thirds of the country's GDP. This includes the country's robust banking industry, the emerging sectors of **information technology**, and tourism.

The dominant force in the German economy is its banking system. Private German banks not only control a substantial stake in German industry but also spread their influence across the globe.

Lufthansa, Germany's national air carrier, carries on its wings another strength of the German economy—tourism. Millions of tourists visit Germany each year. Germany has also built a vibrant trade-fair industry; thousands of visitors use these trade fairs as a window into Europe's markets.

INDUSTRY: THE MAINSTAY OF ECONOMY AND EXPORTS

Heavy industry is still an important part of Germany's economy. Nearly a third of the country's GDP is dependent on the export of machines, motor vehicles, electronics, and chemicals. Supply chains for the steel, coal, cement, and motor vehicle industries are among the most technologically advanced in the world. Germany also has many food and textile enterprises.

The success of Germany's industries is based on the solid infrastructure that Germany has built. The country emphasizes training, both in institutes and the workplace. Research and development is also a major focus area. This has helped Germany engineer world-class products.

The most important branch of Germany's manufacturing sector is the automobile industry. Germany is the third-largest producer of motor vehicles in the world. German-produced vehicles include Volkswagen, BMW, and Porsche. Of the 5.687 million vehicles manufactured in Germany in 1999, 64.6 percent were exported.

The mechanical engineering, plant construction, and electrical engineering industries have contributed to Germany's solid reputation. Well-known names that form a part of the electronics industry include Siemens AG, Bosch Group, and Ruhrkole AG.

The German pharmaceutical industry is among

the oldest and the best in the world. German medicine makers such as Hoechst, Bayer, and BASF are household names all over the world.

AGRICULTURE

Despite thousands of acres of open farmland and forests, Germany is predominantly an urban industrial society. Farming brings in only one percent of the GDP and caters mainly to local needs rather than to exports. Agriculture is heavily subsidized by the EU's Common Agricultural Policy (CAP) and by the German government itself.

ENERGY SOURCES AND TRANSPORTATION

Germany is one of the largest energy consumers. **Lignite** and coal are the principal domestic sources of energy. Environmental protection and resource **conservation** are among the most important factors of Germany's EU-driven energy policy, and it has invested heavily in research into various supplies of renewable energy. **Geothermal** energy sources, solar-power generation, hydroelectricity, as well as **biomass** research are some of the options being explored. In 2002, around 2.9 percent of Germany's energy (10 percent of electricity) was generated in an **eco-friendly** manner, and the country is home to the world's largest solar-power plant. Protecting the enviroment is important to Germany and its people.

TRANSPORTATION

Highways, railways, waterways (both navigable rivers and canals located on modern ports and harbors), and airports make up Germany's complex

Stralau Peninsula in Berlin is the site of urban development that seeks to combine economic, social, and ecological interests.

The roof of the Sony Center looks like an oversized tent pitched above the forum on Potsdamer Platz. The complex was designed by the architect Helmut Jahn for a variety of uses, including residential, work, and entertainment.

transportation system. Germany's airline, Lufthansa, flies around the world and services major international airports.

THE SLOWDOWN

Although Germany's economy is **affluent** and technologically advanced, today the country has one of the slowest-growing economies in all of Europe. Internal and external economic problems slowed the growth rate to less than one percent in 2003–2004.

Germany's internal problems stem from two dominant sources. The first is the unification of West Germany with East Germany, which costs the country more than US$70 billion every year.

The second reason for the country's sluggish economic growth is unemployment and the cost of the country's welfare bill. Germany has the one of the highest unemployment rates in Europe. According to 2004 estimates, more than 10 percent of the population is without a job. With one in ten people unemployed, consumer spending is low, forcing German manufacturers to focus on international markets for their growth. Unemployment and an aging population have pushed social security payments to a level exceeding contributions from workers.

The external problems affecting the German economy include the recession in Europe, which caused a steady fall in the value of the euro, the currency adopted by many nations in the EU. While a weaker euro may mean good news for exports (German products become cheaper and therefore more desirable for the rest of the world), it makes imports more expensive for German consumers. Since Germany relies heavily on imports, a weaker euro creates an economic burden for the nation.

Combined, decreased government income and increased government spending has caused a **deficit** in Germany's treasury. As a result, Germany's deficit is above the 3 percent debt level established by the EU for its member states.

GETTING BACK ON ITS FEET

Germany is trying to overcome its economic depression. The government has begun structural reforms to revive the floundering economy. This corporate restructuring is expected to turn around the country's economy. The government is also looking for new trading partners besides the EU, United States, Switzerland, and Japan.

Among the emerging industries that are helping Germany regain its foothold in world markets is the environment technology industry, which has already captured 18 percent of the world market share. The information and communication technologies industry, the aerospace industry, and the tourism industry are also helping the economy head away from a **deflationary** situation.

Berlin's Waldbuehne Ampitheatre.

4 GERMANY'S PEOPLE AND CULTURE

Germany, home to over 82 million people, is the second most-populated country in Europe. Most Germans are of northern and central European descent. Many can trace their ancestry to ancient tribes such as the Cimbri, Franks, Goths, and Teutons. The country's official language is German.

Quick Facts: The People of Germany

Population: 82,424,609
Ethnic Groups: German 91.5%, Turkish 2.4%, other 6.1%
Age Structure:
> **0–14 years:** 14.7%
> **15–64 years:** 67%
> **65 years and over:** 18.3%

Population Growth Rate: 0.02 %
Birth Rate: 8.45 births/1,000 population
Death Rate: 10.44 deaths/1,000 population
Migration Rate: 2.18 migrant(s)/1,000 population
Infant Mortality Rate: 4.2 deaths/1,000 live births
Life Expectancy at Birth:
> **Total Population:** 78.54 years
> **Male:** 75.56 years
> **Female:** 81.68 years

Total Fertility Rate: 1.38 children born/woman
Religions: Protestant 34%, Roman Catholic 34%, Muslim 3.7%, unaffiliated or other 28.3%
Languages: German
Literacy Rate: 99% (1997 est.)

Note: All figures are from 2004 unless otherwise noted.
Source: www.cia.gov, 2004.

Religion: Freedom of Choice

The German people have full freedom to choose their faith and religion. While 70 percent of the population belong to Christian religions, Islam and Judaism are also practiced. Protestantism is most popular in the north. Roman Catholicism is more prevalent in the south and west. About half the population in what was formerly East Germany has no religious affiliation.

Food and Drink: Sausage, Cake, and Beer

Known for their robust appetites, Germans have traditionally preferred simple, substantial fare. *Frühstück*, the classic German breakfast, consists of breads, rolls, jam, and honey served with coffee and milk. *Mittagessen*, lunch, the main meal of the day, usually consists of meat, potatoes, and vegetables. *Abendbrot*, supper, is generally a cold meal, eaten early. Many Germans often brighten up their afternoons with *kaffe und kuchen*—coffee and cakes.

Non-German-speaking minorities make up 8.5 percent of Germany's population. Native, non-German-speaking groups such as Danes, Frisians, Roma (often called Gypsies), and Sorbs/Wends make up part of this population. Immigrants, such as *"guest workers,"* from Turkey, Italy, and Yugoslavia make up another portion of the non-German-speaking population.

Germans enjoy gathering at street cafés for food and conversation.

Modern lifestyles have brought some changes in eating habits. Germans are cutting back on meat. They enjoy foreign foods such as pizza, pasta, and doner kebabs (a lamb dish). Yet, even today, the old favorites—meat, potatoes, sausages, pickles, bread, and cakes—dominate German cuisine.

Wurst (sausage) and *Aufschnitt* (speciality meat) are the most distinct foods associated with Germany. About 1,500 varieties are available.

An assortment of breads, most made from rye, and rich cakes mark German baking.

As for beverages, most Germans prefer coffee to tea. Beer is the most popular alcoholic drink, followed by wine.

EDUCATION AND SPORTS: A LITERATE AND ACTIVE PEOPLE

Germans take both education and sports very seriously. Almost all adults can read and write, and most can speak at least one foreign language. Nearly half the population plays some form of sport. The country produces great academicians and famous sports figures.

German education is **compulsory** and job oriented. Every child between the ages of six and sixteen must attend school. The school system, though, is quite different from most in North America. To begin, all children attend *Grundschule*, elementary school, until the fourth grade. Then the students are divided into three different school streams. Some children go to *Hauptschule*, a job-oriented school that concentrates on teaching practical skills. Other young people attend *Realschule*, which offers a broader general education. And nearly half the children enroll in the *Gymnasium*, the academic, college-preparatory school. Germany has about sixty universities and many technical and specialized colleges. It has produced great scientists such as Albert Einstein.

When it comes to sports, Germans don't believe in just watching games. They go out and play the games themselves. Soccer is by far the most popular sport. Germany has won the World Cup three times. Tennis, hockey, and basketball also have fans. Bicycling, canoeing, rowing, sailing, swimming, skiing, and hiking are other popular sports.

FESTIVALS AND EVENTS: A FUN-LOVING PEOPLE

Germans really know how to celebrate a holiday. Parades, fancy dress parties, crowds on the streets, floats, shows, and dances—Germany puts on a grand spectacle to mark its festivals and events.

While the country only observes nine religious and two secular holidays nationwide, many festivals and events are celebrated on a regional or even town-specific scale. Many of these holidays are nonreligious. Berlin, for instance, is famous for its film festival. Munich hosts *Oktoberfest*, an annual sixteen-day celebration of beer. *Schultute* is a festival for children. Children are given a schultute—a paper cone full of candy, pencils, and other small gifts—on their first day of first grade.

ARTS AND ARCHITECTURE

Germany's artists rank among the most innovative in Europe in terms of architecture, design, sculpture,

Did You Know?
German Sports Legends
- Boris Becker—tennis
- Steffi Graff—tennis
- Fran Beckenbauer—soccer
- Michael Schumacher—auto racing
- Jan Ullrich—cycling
- Bernhard Langer—golf
- Katja Seizinger—alpine skiing

Pschorr Bräurosl

The Munich Oktoberfest is a sixteen-day celebration of good times and beer.

Schloss Neuschwanstein, a castle in Germany's Bavarian Alps, inspired the designers of Cinderella's castle in Disneyworld.

painting, and printmaking. Huge fortress-like cathedrals, tall churches crowned with pointed arches, and ornate castles decorated with dramatic oil paintings and ***frescoes*** dot the countryside.

Historically, Germany has not only been a leader in architecture; it's also been a leader in painting. Germany gave birth to the expressionist style of painting. George Grosz and Käthe Kollwitz are well-known expressionist artists. Born in the early twentieth century, the expressionist movement sought to express emotions by distorting

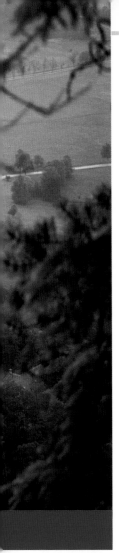

and exaggerating natural forms.

Today, modern **mediums**, such as photography, video art, metal sculpture, environment-driven art, film, and fashion photography, flourish in Germany.

MUSIC AND LITERATURE: A LAND OF GENIUS

Having produced numerous great poets, thinkers, and musical **virtuosos**, Germany can truly be called a land of genius.

In literature, the first well-recognized German work was Martin Luther's sixteenth-century translation of the Bible. The greatest period for German literature lasted from about 1750 to 1830. Greats such as Johann Wolfgang von Goethe, Friedrich Schiller, and Friedrich Holderlin were the leading authors of this period. Later German writers Thomas Mann, Hermann Hesse, Heinrich Böll, and Günter Grass have all received the Nobel Prize for Literature.

Germany enjoys a special place in children's literature. The Grimm Brothers traveled the German countryside, recording what have become some of the world's best-loved fairy-tales. Characters such as Hansel and Gretel, the Pied Piper of Hamelin, and Cinderella were all based on German folk-tales.

Johann Sebastian Bach established the great tradition of German music in the early 1700s. Ludwig von Beethoven was the virtuoso of the 1800s. Felix Mendelssohn, Franz Schubert, Robert Schumann, Richard Wagner, Richard Strauss, Arnold Schoenburg, and Kurt Weill, all great composers, carried the baton through to the twentieth century. Works by these classical composers continue to be enjoyed the world over. However, Germans today enjoy a wide variety of music, including hip-hop, rock, and pop.

Shell Haus in Berlin is an example of Germany's modern architecture.

5 THE CITIES

Today's Germany is an extremely urban society. Over 80 percent of its population live in cities and towns. Most Germans earn a fairly comfortable income and lead prosperous lifestyles. Urban German families tend to be quite small; German couples usually have only one child, and many have none at all.

Most of Germany's cities are medium-sized or small; only a few large cities exist. A majority of German cities were founded centuries ago. Today, they offer their residents every modern convenience yet maintain their medieval character. Castles, stately timbered homes, cathedrals, **abbeys**, romantic winding streets, and even Roman ruins merge with modern structures to give German towns a unique identity that blends old and new.

German cities also consciously promote a rich cultural life. Many towns subsidize theater, opera, music festivals, and galleries.

VARIED POPULATION DENSITY

Germany is comprised of sixteen states (*Länder*) whose population densities vary greatly. The most densely populated are urban states like Berlin, Hamburg, and Bremen. The least densely populated are Mecklenburg-West Pomerania and Brandenburg, both mostly rural. The state with the largest population, one-fifth of the nation's total, is North Rhine-Westphalia. This state has many industrial cities. The largest state, Bavaria, has a low population density. Its capital, Munich, however, is a crowded urban center.

BERLIN: THE CAPITAL

Berlin is Germany's capital and most-populated city. After World War II, the Berlin Wall divided it into two cities, East Berlin and West Berlin. Today, reunited Berlin is an acknowledged seat of culture. It hosts events such as the Jazz Festival and the International Film Festival. It is home to more than 170 museums, including Europe's largest museum complex, Museum Island. Berlin also boasts extensive woodlands and rivers that **meander** through the city. One park, Volkspark Prenzlauer Berg, is built on a mountain of rubble.

HAMBURG: A RICH METROPOLIS

Germany's second-most populated city, Hamburg, is one of the richest **metropolises** in Europe. Its wealth is a result of its thriving harbor and powerful media industry. A grid of narrow canals and three rivers—the Elbe, Alster, and Bille—shapes the city's port. Each year, about 12,000 ships move some 70 million tons of goods, making Hamburg the most important port in Germany and one of the largest harbors in Europe. Because of its coastal location, Hamburg has also attracted immigrants from all over Europe, who make up 15 to 20 percent of its population.

MUNICH: BMW LAND

Situated in the southern state of Bavaria, Munich is one of Germany's leading industrial cities and the headquarters of world famous car manufacturer BMW (*Bayerische Motoren Werke* [Bavarian Motor Works]). The city is proud of its many museums and splendid architecture.

Munich's Oktoberfest is hailed as the world's largest fair. Also called the *Wiesn*, the Oktoberfest is an annual celebration of beer. People from all

The Museum Kommunikation

Berlin's Brandenburg Gate is a famous tourist attraction.

over the world come to enjoy sausages and sample the beverages on tap in the many beer tents. The good times last for sixteen days.

THE RHINE-RUHR AREA: AN INDUSTRIAL HUB

Crowded urban centers have also developed in industrial areas. The Rhine-Ruhr area, the center of German heavy industry, is a vast population hub. Five large cities—Düsseldorf, Duisburg, Dortmund, Essen, and Cologne—make up the Ruhr area. Many people live in adjacent areas or towns and commute to the cities, so these urban centers service far more people than those living within the city limits.

BREMEN: A HARBOR CITY

Though Hamburg is Germany's largest harbor city, Bremen is the most important economically. It houses one of the world's most modern container terminals and handles nearly 1.3 million crates annually. The German Maritime Museum, with its collection of five hundred ship models, is a favorite site for visitors to Bremen. Germany's ever-increasing aerospace industry also has a strong base in Bremen.

ENCHANTING TOWNS: XANTEN AND LINDAU

One of Germany's oldest towns, Xanten dates back to around 100 CE. One of the biggest Roman settlements was located here. Today, this town of picturesque medieval streets, all built around thousand-year-old St. Viktor's Cathedral, combines *cosmopolitan* flair with an easygoing country attitude.

Lindau is a holiday town. Located on an island in Lake Constance, where Germany, Austria, and Switzerland meet, Lindau offers a spectacular view of the Alps and has a carefully preserved medieval town center. Cities like these make Germany a unique and valuable member of the European Union.

The EU flag

6

THE FORMATION OF THE EUROPEAN UNION

The EU is an economic and political confederation of twenty-five European nations. Member countries abide by common foreign and security policies and cooperate on judicial and domestic affairs. The confederation, however, does not replace existing states or governments. Each of the twenty-five member states is *autonomous*, but they have all agreed to establish some common institutions and to hand over some of their own decision-making powers to these international bodies. As a result, decisions on matters that interest all member states can be made democratically, accommodating everyone's concerns and interests.

Today, the EU is the most powerful regional organization in the world. It has evolved from a primarily economic organization to an increasingly political one. Besides promoting economic cooperation, the EU requires that its members uphold fundamental values of peace and **solidarity**, human dignity, freedom, and equality. Based on the principles of democracy and the rule of law, the EU respects the culture and organizations of member states.

HISTORY

The seeds of the EU were planted more than fifty years ago in a Europe reduced to smoking piles of rubble by two world wars. European nations suffered great financial difficulties in the postwar period. They were struggling to get back on their feet and realized that another war would cause further hardship. Knowing that internal conflict was hurting all of Europe, a drive began toward European cooperation.

France took the first historic step. On May 9, 1950 (now celebrated as Europe Day), Robert Schuman, the French foreign minister, proposed the coal and steel industries of France and West Germany be coordinated under a single supranational authority. The proposal, known as the Treaty of Paris, attracted four other countries—Belgium, Luxembourg, the Netherlands, and Italy—and resulted in the 1951 formation of the European Coal and Steel Community (ECSC). These six countries became the founding members of the EU.

In 1957, European cooperation took its next big leap. Under the Treaty of Rome, the European Economic Community (EEC) and the European Atomic Energy Community (EURATOM) were formed. Informally known as the Common Market, the EEC promoted joining the national economies into a single European economy. The 1965 Treaty of Brussels (more commonly referred to as the Merger Treaty) united these various treaty organizations under a single umbrella, the European Community (EC).

In 1992, the Maastricht Treaty (also known as the Treaty of the European Union) was signed in Maastricht, the Netherlands, signaling the birth of the EU as it stands today. **Ratified** the following year, the Maastricht Treaty provided for a central banking system, a common currency (the euro) to replace the national currencies, a legal definition of the EU, and a framework for expanding the

The EU's united economy has allowed it to become a worldwide financial power.

EU's political role, particularly in the area of foreign and security policy.

By 1993, the member countries completed their move toward a single market and agreed to participate in a larger common market, the European Economic Area, established in 1994.

The EU, headquartered in Brussels, Belgium, reached its current member strength in spurts. In

© BCE ECB EZB EKT EKP 2002

200

© BCE ECB EZB EKT EKP 2002

100

© BCE ECB EZB EKT EKP 2002

50

© BCE ECB EZB EKT EKP 2002

The euro, the EU's currency

1973, Denmark, Ireland, and the United Kingdom joined the six founding members of the EC. They were followed by Greece in 1981, and Portugal and Spain in 1986. The 1990s saw the unification of the two Germanys, and as a result, East Germany entered the EU fold. Austria, Finland, and Sweden joined the EU in 1995, bringing the total number of member states to fifteen. In 2004, the EU nearly doubled its size when ten countries—Cyprus, the Czech Republic, Estonia, Hungary, Latvia, Lithuania, Malta, Poland, Slovakia, and Slovenia—became members.

The EU Framework

The EU's structure has often been compared to a "roof of a temple with three columns." As established by the Maastricht Treaty, this three-pillar framework encompasses all the policy areas—or pillars—of European cooperation. The three pillars of the EU are the European Community, the Common Foreign and Security Policy (CFSP), and Police and Judicial Co-operation in Criminal Matters.

Quick Facts: The European Union

Number of Member Countries: 25
Official Languages: 20—Czech, Danish, Dutch, English, Estonian, Finnish, French, German, Greek, Hungarian, Italian, Latvian, Lithuanian, Maltese, Polish, Portuguese, Slovak, Slovenian, Spanish, and Swedish; additional language for treaty purposes: Irish Gaelic.
Motto: *In Varietate Concordia* (United in Diversity)
European Council's President: Each member state takes a turn to lead the council's activities for 6 months.
European Commission's President: José Manuel Barroso (Portugal)
European Parliament's President: Josep Borrell (Spain)
Total Area: 1,502,966 square miles (3,892,685 sq. km.)
Population: 454,900,000
Population Density: 302.7 people/square mile (116.8 people/sq. km.)
GDP: €9.61.1012
Per Capita GDP: €21,125
Formation:
- Declared: February 7, 1992, with signing of the Maastricht Treaty
- Recognized: November 1, 1993, with the ratification of the Maastricht Treaty

Community Currency: Euro. Currently 12 of the 25 member states have adopted the euro as their currency.
Anthem: "Ode to Joy"
Flag: Blue background with 12 gold stars arranged in a circle
Official Day: Europe Day, May 9.

Source: europa.eu.int

PILLAR ONE

The European Community pillar deals with economic, social, and environmental policies. It is a body consisting of the European Parliament, European Commission, European Court of Justice, Council of the European Union, and the European Courts of Auditors.

PILLAR TWO

The idea that the EU should speak with one voice in world affairs is as old as the European integration process itself. Toward this end, the Common Foreign and Security Policy (CFSP) was formed in 1993.

PILLAR THREE

The cooperation of EU member states in judicial and criminal matters ensures that its citizens enjoy the freedom to travel, work, and live securely and safely anywhere within the EU. The third pillar—Police and Judicial Co-operation in Criminal Matters—helps to protect EU citizens from international crime and to ensure equal access to justice and fundamental rights across the EU.

The flags of the EU's nations:

top row, left to right
Belgium, the Czech Republic, Denmark, Germany, Estonia, Greece

second row, left to right
Spain, France, Ireland, Italy, Cyprus, Latvia

third row, left to right
Lithuania, Luxembourg, Hungary, Malta, the Netherlands, Austria

bottom row, left to right
Poland, Portugal, Slovenia, Slovakia, Finland, Sweden, United Kingdom

ECONOMIC STATUS

As of May 2004, the EU had the largest economy in the world, followed closely by the United States. But even though the EU continues to enjoy a trade surplus, it faces the twin problems of high unemployment rates and **stagnancy**.

The 2004 addition of ten new member states is expected to boost economic growth. EU membership is likely to stimulate the economies of these relatively poor countries. In turn, their prosperity growth will be beneficial to the EU.

THE EURO

The EU's official currency is the euro, which came into circulation on January 1, 2002. The shift to the euro has been the largest monetary changeover in the world. Twelve countries—Belgium, Germany, Greece, Spain, France, Ireland, Italy, Luxembourg, the Netherlands, Finland, Portugal, and Austria—have adopted it as their currency.

SINGLE MARKET

Within the EU, laws of member states are harmonized and domestic policies are coordinated to create a larger, more-efficient single market.

The chief features of the EU's internal policy on the single market are:

- free trade of goods and services

- a common EU competition law that controls anticompetitive activities of companies and member states

- removal of internal border control and harmonization of external controls between member states

- freedom for citizens to live and work anywhere in the EU as long as they are not dependent on the state

- free movement of *capital* between member states

- harmonization of government regulations, corporation law, and trademark registration

- a single currency

- coordination of environmental policy

- a common agricultural policy and a common fisheries policy

- a common system of indirect taxation, the value-added tax (VAT), and common customs duties and *excise*

- funding for research

- funding for aid to disadvantaged regions

The EU's external policy on the single market specifies:

- a common external *tariff* and a common position in international trade negotiations

- funding of programs in other Eastern European countries and developing countries

COOPERATION AREAS

EU member states cooperate in other areas as well. Member states can vote in European Parliament elections. Intelligence sharing and cooperation in criminal matters are carried out through EUROPOL and the Schengen Information System.

The EU is working to develop common foreign and security policies. Many member states are resisting such a move, however, saying these are sensitive areas best left to individual member states. Arguing in favor of a common approach to security and foreign policy are countries like France and Germany, who insist that a safer and more secure Europe can only become a reality under the EU umbrella.

One of the EU's great achievements has been to create a boundary-free area within which people, goods, services, and money can move around freely; this ease of movement is sometimes called "the four freedoms." As the EU grows in size, so do the challenges facing it—and yet its fifty-year history has amply demonstrated the power of cooperation.

Europe is proud of its "bright idea," a union with economic and political power.

The EU believes that it can use its power to act as a "lighthouse" for the rest of the world.

KEY EU INSTITUTIONS

Five key institutions play a specific role in the EU.

THE EUROPEAN PARLIAMENT

The European Parliament (EP) is the democratic voice of the people of Europe. Directly elected every five years, the Members of the European Parliament (MEPs) sit not in national **blocs** but in political groups representing the seven main political parties of the member states. Each group reflects the political ideology of the national parties to which its members belong. Some MEPs are not attached to any political group.

COUNCIL OF THE EUROPEAN UNION

The Council of the European Union (formerly known as the Council of Ministers) is the main leg-

islative and decision-making body in the EU. It brings together the nationally elected representatives of the member-state governments. One minister from each of the EU's member states attends council meetings. It is the forum in which government representatives can assert their interests and reach compromises. Increasingly, the Council of the European Union and the EP are acting together as colegislators in decision-making processes.

European Commission

The European Commission does much of the day-to-day work of the EU. Politically independent, the commission represents the interests of the EU as a whole, rather than those of individual member states. It drafts proposals for new European laws, which it presents to the EP and the Council of the European Union. The European Commission makes sure EU decisions are implemented properly and supervises the way EU funds are spent. It also sees that everyone abides by the European treaties and European law.

The EU member-state governments choose the European Commission president, who is then approved by the EP. Member states, in consultation with the incoming president, nominate the other European Commission members, who must also be approved by the EP. The commission is appointed for a five-year term, but can be dismissed by the EP. Many members of its staff work in Brussels, Belgium.

Court of Justice

Headquartered in Luxembourg, the Court of Justice of the European Communities consists of one independent judge from each EU country. This court ensures that the common rules decided in the EU are understood and followed uniformly by all the members. The Court of Justice settles disputes over how EU treaties and legislation are interpreted. If national courts are in doubt about how to apply EU rules, they must ask the Court of Justice. Individuals can also bring proceedings against EU institutions before the court.

Court of Auditors

EU funds must be used legally, economically, and for their intended purpose. The Court of Auditors, an independent EU institution located in Luxembourg, is responsible for overseeing how EU money is spent. In effect, these auditors help European taxpayers get better value for the money that has been channeled into the EU.

Other Important Bodies

1. European Economic and Social Committee: expresses the opinions of organized civil society on economic and social issues

2. Committee of the Regions: expresses the opinions of regional and local authorities

3. European Central Bank: responsible for monetary policy and managing the euro

4. European Ombudsman: deals with citizens' complaints about mismanagement by any EU institution or body

5. European Investment Bank: helps achieve EU objectives by financing investment projects

Together with a number of agencies and other bodies completing the system, the EU's institutions have made it the most powerful organization in the world.

EU Member States

In order to become a member of the EU, a country must have a stable democracy that guarantees the rule of law, human rights, and protection of minorities. It must also have a functioning market economy as well as a civil service capable of applying and managing EU laws.

The EU provides substantial financial assistance and advice to help candidate countries prepare themselves for membership. As of October 2004, the EU has twenty-five member states. Bulgaria and Romania are likely to join in 2007, which would bring the EU's total population to nearly 500 million.

In December 2004, the EU decided to open negotiations with Turkey on its proposed membership. Turkey's possible entry into the EU has been fraught with controversy. Much of this controversy has centered on Turkey's human rights record and the divided island of Cyprus. If allowed to join the EU, Turkey would be its most-populous member state.

The 2004 expansion was the EU's most ambitious enlargement to date. Never before has the EU embraced so many new countries, grown so much in terms of area and population, or encompassed so many different histories and cultures. As the EU moves forward into the twenty-first century, it will undoubtedly continue to grow in both political and economic strength.

7 GERMANY IN THE EUROPEAN UNION

If the EU were a person, the Federal Republic of
Germany could truly be called its heart. A few de-

GERMANY'S PLACE IN EU HISTORY

Fifty years ago, when France first pushed forward the idea of European cooperation, Germany reached out to take France's hand in cooperation and friendship. That historic handshake brought together two nations, once on opposite sides of a bitter war, to work for a mutually beneficial future. When Belgium, Luxembourg, the Netherlands, and Italy joined Germany and France, the foundation was laid for the development of the largest union in the world. It also marked the beginning of a new Germany, a country determined to do what was necessary to heal the wounds of the past and give the children of the world a peaceful and prosperous future.

THE HEART OF EU

Germany can be called the heart of EU for many reasons. In addition to its central geographic location, the country has functioned politically as a driving force for European unification. It supports greater cooperation within the EU, with economic and political **integration**, a more unified foreign and defense policy, and increased independence from the United States. Germany is one of the EU's strongest supporters of supranationalism—a governmental approach in which EU member states would have to give up some decision-making control to appointed officials or elected representatives and in which decisions would be based on "majority rules."

Britain and some of the newer EU members oppose Germany's vision of Europe. They want to surrender a minimum of **sovereignty**, especially over such things as taxation, defense, and foreign affairs. They are anxious to maintain close links with the United States. They are against supranationalism, instead favoring intergovernmentalism—a governmental approach in which member states must reach unanimous agreement before moving ahead on decisions.

Financially, the EU's fortunes are influenced greatly by the ebb and flow of the German economy. With a GDP of $2.271 trillion, Germany is the largest economy in the eurozone, the twelve countries that have adopted the euro as their currency. Germany is also the largest contributor to the EU budget.

A BALANCING ACT

As an EU member, Germany, the nation-state, has had to concede some of its rights. Although the country has its own laws and rules, it is so closely tied to the EU that it is no longer able to act independently in many areas.

For instance, Germany no longer acts alone in international economic matters. Now it usually acts through Europe. Germany also increasingly

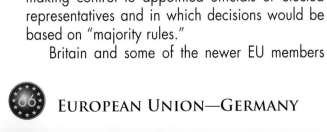

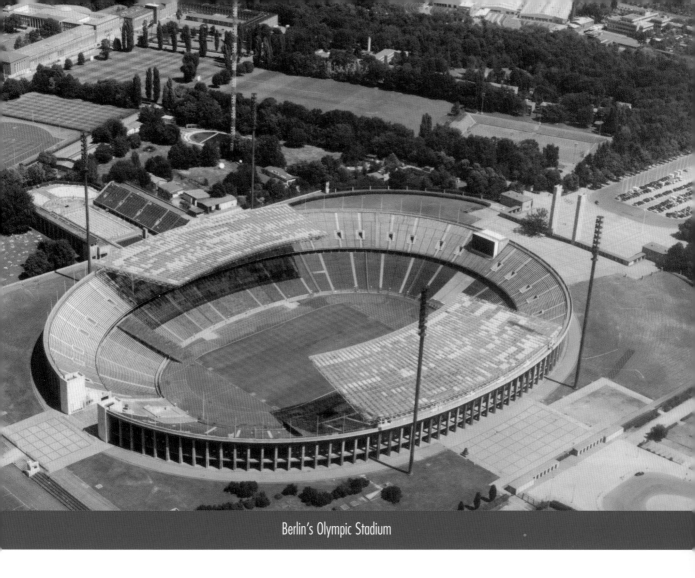

Berlin's Olympic Stadium

makes its international policies in conjunction and consultation with other EU members.

The challenge for today's Germany is to strike the right balance between domestic and EU responsibilities. Take for example Germany's welfare policy. Germany has always had a generous social welfare policy toward its unemployed. This welfare policy places a great strain on the country's finances. Though the country is willing to bear the financial burden, it is under pressure from the EU to trim its budget. However, the country won't compromise by reducing welfare programs.

LOBBYING FOR LOWER TRADE BARRIERS

Germany is one of the world's largest trading nations, ranking second only to the United States; one in every four jobs in Germany depends on foreign trade. The country's economy has traditionally been driven by exports, since the factories of both East Germany and West Germany always produced more than could be sold in the domestic market. Even after unification, the German economy has had to look beyond its borders.

The country's most important trading partners are its fellow EU members, as well as the United States, Switzerland, and Japan. Since EU members account for over half of German trade, the

Constructing the modern Potsdamer Platz metrocenter in Berlin.

creation of a single market has greatly benefited the country. Now Germany is pushing the EU to reduce trade barriers that prevent developing countries from marketing their goods in EU member countries. Currently, developing countries wanting to export their goods to EU nations have to pay taxes, which in some cases are quite high. Often, they cannot sell more than a specified amount to the EU nation, since the latter has fixed a **quota** for imports.

Germany wants these trade barriers eliminated. Once they are removed, the developing countries would have to grant greater access to EU nations. This would work in Germany's favor, since the country needs to find buyers for its excess goods.

ACTIVE SUPPORT FOR CAP

Although Germany is not a major agricultural state like Spain and France, it is an active supporter of the EU's CAP. The program's aim is to provide farmers with a reasonable standard of living and give consumers quality food at fair prices. Today, CAP's focus is food safety, preserving of the rural environment, and stabilizing the value of money.

Although modernization of farms, rural development, and more equitable payments to farmers have been on the top of the EU agenda, other concerns have begun to push their way forward. More intensive farming methods have sparked concerns that the environment and animal welfare are not getting the attention they deserve. Consumers feared these methods were to blame for mad cow disease, the chemical dioxin in milk, artificial hormones in meat, and other food-related health scares. Consequently, production **subsidies** are being sharply curtailed in favor of direct payments to farmers. To be eligible for such payments, however, one must comply with rules on the environment, animal welfare, hygiene standards, and preservation of the countryside.

All of these changes have sound scientific foundations. The EU funds much research into **sustainable** production, careful use of natural resources, and plant and animal diseases. As one of the largest importers of agricultural produce in Europe, Germany has reasons to support the EU's **stringent** standards on agricultural products.

EU ENLARGEMENT AND GERMAN CONCERNS

The EU enlargement has dealt Germany a twin blow by placing a financial burden on the country and creating competition from within the EU.

Many of the smaller Eastern European countries that joined the EU in 2004 are relatively poor compared to their Western European counterparts. Countries like Cyprus, the Czech Republic,

The world clock in Berlin shows the time around the world.

Estonia, Hungary, Latvia, Lithuania, Malta, Poland, Slovakia, and Slovenia have relatively weak infrastructures, and few world-class companies are willing to invest there.

For infrastructure development and improvement, these countries are turning to the EU for financial assistance. To increase investment in their countries, they have set very low corporate tax levels to attract companies to set up offices and factories in their cities.

Given this scenario, Germany's loss is twofold. First, attracted by the low taxes in neighboring countries, large corporations are considering shifting their factories out of Germany. Such a move would rattle the spine of Germany's economy. Second, not only does Germany lose business to its poorer neighbors, it indirectly ends up financing the building of infrastructure in these less-affluent countries.

To provide for the needs of the new member countries, the EU has asked richer nations to increase their budget contributions, and since Germany is the largest contributor to the EU budget, the demand places a great burden on that country. Also, the EU is redirecting some aid from former East Germany to the new EU members. The EU has been providing substantial funds and subsidies to aid development within East Germany. According to the news service Bloomberg, some 17.9 billion euros (US$22.2 billion) of subsidies will flow to East Germany between 2000 and 2006. But with the addition of ten new, relatively poor member states, the EC intends to cut the subsidies provided to the states of East Germany by 60 percent. The EC is also planning to reduce subsidies given to companies that set up offices in East Germany. This aid will also be used to assist the poorer regions of the expanded EU.

In an interview with the economic daily *Handelsblatt* and the *Wall Street Journal Europe*, Germany's chancellor, Gerhard Schroeder, termed the situation "***fiscal*** dumping." "We must be careful of a one-way fiscal competition to the detriment of net contributors to the EU budget," Schroeder told lawmakers in Berlin. He went on to suggest that the new members of the EU must agree to a "tax corridor"—a minimum level of taxes across the EU states—to give all member states an equal opportunity to attract outside investment.

THE WAY FORWARD

While member states zealously guard their sovereignty and interests, Europeans cannot deny that the Common Market, the EC, and now the EU have greatly improved their lives, their security, and their role in world affairs. The sustained efforts to set up a common customs union for all EU member states, reduced trade barriers, and common standards for goods and services that can be sold within the EU have begun to reap benefits for Germany as well as the rest of Europe.

Despite greater competition in world markets, German exports have increased substantially. In addition, the continuous rise in direct investments by international companies in Germany and by German companies abroad shows just how strong the German economy is when compared to its international competitors.

The city of Heidelberg

As Germany pushes for the harmonization of laws across the EU, it is faced with resistance from countries such as Britain and Ireland that have low corporate tax rates. Since all EU decisions must be unanimous, Germany is considering moving ahead with like-minded countries and harmonizing its tax laws. In such a situation, one could well see an EU that operates at several levels or speeds, with nations choosing the paths most suitable to them.

A Calendar of German Festivals

Germany celebrates many religious, historical, and nonreligious festivals. Food, fun, parades, and dancing are integral parts of most German festivals.

January: January 1 is a public holiday. The **New Year** festivities traditionally include champagne and fireworks. **Epiphany**, celebrated on January 6, primarily in Bavaria, Baden-Wuttenrnberg, and Saxony Anhalt, marks the end of the Christmas season. On this day, children dress up as the Three Wise Men and go door to door collecting money for charity and receiving candies as their reward.

February: February is the carnival month. In Germany, the season of Carnival is referred to as **Karneval**, **Fastnacht**, or **Fasching** depending on the region. Carnivals take place during the fasting period before **Lent**. People use this time as a last opportunity to drink, eat, and frolic before the sacrifices of Lent. Costumed street parties and parades are the highlights of the Karneval. Carnivals in Cologne, Frankfurt, and Mainz are particularly famous. Berlin also hosts a very important **International Film Festival** in February.

March/April: Easter Week may fall in March or April, and the festival is celebrated throughout the country. In Germany, **Easter** begins with covering the Cross on **Good Friday**. On this day Germans traditionally eat fish dishes. Easter Mass starts on Saturday evening and continues until Sunday morning. Sunday is **Family Day**. German families enjoy a special Easter lunch. Colored eggs and a lamb-shaped cake decorate the table.

May: Maifest is celebrated on the eve of May 1. This festival signifies the end of winter and is accompanied by singing and dancing in traditional clothes. May 1 is **Tag der Arbeit**, Labor Day. **Ascension Day** and **Pentecost**, religious festivals, fall in the May–June period.

June: Catholics in Germany celebrate **Fronleichnam**, Corpus Christi. **St. Johannistag** is another religious holiday. A midsummer festival, it honors St. John the Baptist. The themes of the festival are light and warmth. These celebrations have their roots in pre-Christian times when people used to celebrate such themes with midsummer bonfires, which young men and women leaped over. It was said that the summer's crops would grow as high as the leapers were able to jump.

July: This is the time for all marksmen to show off their shooting skills at shooting festivals organized across the country. The Love Parade in Berlin is a unique festival that has taken place in early July since 1989. It attracts almost two million people. Basically a big music festival, it began as a celebration of the love that came about between East Germany and West Germany with the destruction of the Berlin Wall.

August: The Catholic festival celebrating **Assumption Day** occurs on August 15. **Weinfeste** is a celebration of wine. Wine festivals are held across the Rhine-Mosel belt beginning in August. As soon as the grapes have been picked, it's time for parades, fireworks, the crowning of wine queens, and wine tasting.

September: Oktoberfest, held in the city of Munich, starts in September and extends into October. The sixteen-day festival pays tribute to beer, the most popular drink in Germany. The festival began as a wedding celebration in 1810, when Princess Therese married Bavarian Crown Prince Ludwig. Today it attracts people from all over the world. On the opening day, as the clock of St. Paul's Church in Munich strikes noon, the first cask of beer is tapped and the first glass is drunk to a twelve-cannon salute. The festival then comes alive, and beer tents dot the entire city.

October: October 3 is **German Unity Day**, a celebration of the Workers' Uprising of 1953 in East Germany. It has been a national holiday since 1990. **Erntedankfest**, the German Thanksgiving, is celebrated on the first Sunday of October. Beautiful displays, typically of colorful fruit and vegetables as well as grains and breads, are set up before the altar as symbols of gratitude to God. **Reformation Day** is observed on October 31 in certain parts of the country.

November: All Saints' Day on November 1 is an important religious holiday in certain parts of the country. People remember and honor the dead on this day. **St. Martinstag**, celebrated November 10–11, remembers Martin of Tours, a very popular fourth-century saint known for his humility and generosity. A procession of lights is made to celebrate St. Martinstag. **Advent** signals the start of the Christmas season. Advent begins on the first Sunday after November 26, and is celebrated every Sunday until Christmas Eve. Christmas markets open with the start of Advent. Holly wreaths with four candles are displayed on tables in homes across Germany. One candle is lit each Sunday until the last is lit on Christmas Day.

December: On December 5, the eve of **Nickloustag**, the German Santa, St. Nicklaus, visits children. Children place their boots outside the door or by the fireplace. Good children get toys and sweets in their boots; bad ones get twigs. **Christmas Day**, December 25, is family time in Germany symbolized by the krippe, models of Jesus's birth in a stable. The German New Year's eve is called **Silvester** in honor of the fourth-century pope under whom the Romans adopted Christianity. This is the time for all-night parties and fireworks.

Zwetschgenkuchen
(Plum Cake)

This classic German pastry is a delicious way to use all the plums that ripen in late summer. Serve it with lots of fresh whipped cream.

Makes 6 servings

Ingredients

Pastry
1/2 cup margarine or butter
2 cups all-purpose flour
1/4 cup sugar
1 teaspoon baking powder
1/2 teaspoon salt
1/2 teaspoon grated lemon peel
1/4 teaspoon ground mace
1 egg, beaten
2 tablespoons cold water

Topping
2 pounds purple or red plums, halved and pitted
    (about 5 cups)
3/4 cup sugar
2 tablespoons flour
1 teaspoon ground cinnamon
1/4 cup slivered almonds

Directions
Prepare pastry: Cut margarine into flour, sugar, baking powder, salt, lemon peel, and mace until mixture resembles fine crumbs. Mix egg and water; stir into flour mixture. Gather pastry into a ball; knead just until smooth, 5 or 6 times. Press evenly on bottom and side of ungreased 9-inch round pan.

Place plum halves cut sides down and overlapping slightly in pastry-lined pan. Mix sugar, flour, and cinnamon; sprinkle over plums. Sprinkle with almonds. Bake in 375° oven until pastry is golden brown and plums are bubbly, 35 to 40 minutes.

Mandelflammerimit Erdbeeren
(Almond Pudding with Strawberries)

This dessert is a favorite among school-age children.

Serves 6–8

Ingredients
1 cup, plus 2 tablespoons ground almonds
1 quart plus 3 tablespoons milk, plus 3 additional tablespoons cold milk
1/3 cup, plus 1 tablespoon sugar
2–3 tablespoons rosewater
pinch of salt
3 tablespoons cornstarch or arrowroot
1 teaspoon almond extract
fresh strawberries, washed, hulled, and dusted
    with confectioners' sugar

Directions

Place ground almonds and milk in a heavy pot over low heat and bring to a low boil. Stir in sugar, rosewater, and salt. In a small bowl, dissolve cornstarch or arrowroot in 3 tablespoons cold milk, then add to almond mixture. Stirring constantly, allow mixture to boil until it thickens. (It won't reach its full thickening until it has reached a boil, so don't cut short this step.) Thoroughly stir in almond extract. Pour into a glass serving bowl and cool for several hours. Decorate with strawberries and serve.

Gurken und Kartoffelsuppe (Potato and Cucumber Soup)

Served hot, this soup is wonderful accompanied with thick slices of bread.

Serves 4

Ingredients

4 medium potatoes, peeled and diced
2 teaspoons salt
2 cups cold water
1/4 teaspoon white pepper
1 cup heavy cream
1/2 cup milk
1 green onion, grated
1 tablespoon chopped fresh dill

Directions

Peel the cucumber and slice it lengthwise. Scoop out and discard seeds; dice cucumber. In a heavy 2 1/2-quart saucepan, boil potatoes in 2 cups salted water until the potatoes are very soft. Using an electric hand mixer, blend potatoes into their cooking liquid. Stir in pepper, cream, milk, grated onion, and the cucumber. Simmer gently until cucumber is tender (about 5 minutes). Serve hot.

Potato Skin Soup

Serves 6

Ingredients

Peelings of 2 pounds of potatoes (don't peel too thinly)
1 onion chopped
4 tablespoons butter
4 cups chicken stock
Light cream (half-and-half) if necessary
Parsley or chives to garnish

Directions

Melt the butter in a large pot over medium heat. Add the potato peelings and onion; cook until tender. Add the stock and bring to a boil. Remove from heat and pour into blender; process on high until smooth. Reheat, and add cream if too thick. Pour into soup bowls, and garnish with parsley or chives.

Project and Report Ideas

Maps

- Make a map of the eurozone, and create a legend to indicate key manufacturing industries throughout the EU.
- Create an export map of Germany using a legend to represent all the major products exported by Germany. The map should clearly indicate all of Germany's industrial regions.

Reports

- Write a brief report on Germany's automobile industry.
- The German automobile manufacturer BMW traces its history to the turbulent time of Nazi rule in Germany. Write a report on the history of BMW and the role it played during World War II.
- Write a report on Germany's concerns within the EU.
- Write a brief report on any of the following historical events: World War I, World War II, the unification of Germany.

Biographies

Write a one-page biography on one of the following:

- Michael Schumacher
- Adolf Hitler
- Johann Sebastian Bach
- Käthe Kollwitz

Journal

- Imagine you are a student in Germany who is finishing primary school. Write a journal about the three different school options open to you. Each one has some advantages. You are not sure what to do. Finally you make a choice. Your journal should tell why you have chosen that option.

- Read more about artist Käthe Kollwitz. Imagine you are Käthe Kollwitz. Life is hard for you in wartime Germany, but you stay. Write a journal about your life and what makes you stay in the country while other artists are leaving.

Projects

- Learn the German expressions for simple words such as hello, good day, please, thank you. Try them on your friends.
- Make a calendar of your country's festivals and list the ones that are common or similar in Germany. Are they celebrated differently in Germany? If so, how?
- Go online or to the library and find images of Gothic churches. Create a model of one.
- Make a poster showing German cars or airplanes used in the world wars.
- Make a list of all the rivers, places, seas, and islands that you have read about in this book and indicate them on a map of Germany.
- Find a German recipe other than the ones given in this book, and ask an adult to help you make it. Share it with members of your class.
- Read a Brothers Grimm tale and create your own fairy tale.
- Learn about the Expressionist art movement, and create a work of art in that manner.

Group Activities

- Debate: One side should take the role of Germany and the other Britain. Germany's position is that EU should adopt a supranational approach, while Britain will speak in favor of the intergovernmental mode.
- Role play: Reenact the scene of the Berlin Wall coming down.

Chronology

1000 BCE	Tribes from northern Europe take over large portions of the land that is now Germany.
800 CE	Charlemagne's empire is established.
962 CE	Otto I is crowned emperor and establishes the Holy Roman Empire.
1517	The Reformation begins in Germany.
1618	A protest by Bohemian Protestants in Prague marks the beginning of the Thirty Years' War.
1648	The Peace of Westphalia ends the Thirty Years' War.
1792	The war against revolutionary France begins.
1803	Germany is redistributed.
1806	The Holy Roman Empire of the German Nation is dissolved.
1813–1815	Liberation wars against Napoleonic France begin.
1815	The German Confederation Holy Alliance between Russia, Austria, and Prussia is founded to suppress liberal movements.
1862	Otto von Bismarck is appointed prime minister of Prussia.
1870–1871	Franco-German War is waged.
1871	The German Empire is founded with Bismarck as chancellor. Emperor William I is crowned in Versailles.
1914	World War I begins.
1918	Germany is defeated in World War I.
1919	A German national assembly is elected to write a constitution, and the Weimar Republic is established.
1933	Adolf Hitler is appointed chancellor.
1935	Anti-Semitic "Nuremberg Laws" are passed.
1939	Germany invades Poland, and World War II begins.
1945	The Allies defeat Germany in World War II.
1948–1949	The Soviet Union institutes an economic blockade of West Berlin; it fails.
1949	The Federal Republic of Germany is founded and a constitution established.
1953	The Soviet Union crushes an East German revolt.
1957	The European Economic Community begins between Germany, France, Belgium, Italy, Luxembourg, and the Netherlands.
1961	The Soviets build the Berlin Wall to prevent East Germans from crossing to West Germany.
1989	East Germany opens the Berlin Wall and other barriers.
1990	East and West Germany unify and become a single entity again.
1992	The Maastricht Treaty is signed, creating the EU.
1997	Germany signs the new EU Treaty, the Treaty of Amsterdam.
2001	Germany's parliament condemns the terrorist attacks of September 11 in the United States and endorses Germany's solidarity with the United States.
2002	Euro notes and coins replace the deutsche mark.

FURTHER READING/INTERNET RESOURCES

Ayer, Eleanor H., Helen Waterford, and Alfons Heck. *Parallel Journeys.* New York: Simon & Schuster, 1995.
Lane, Kathyrn. *Germany, the Culture.* New York: Crabtree, 2001.
Nickles, Greg, and Niki Walker. *Germany.* New York: Raintree Steck-Vaughn, 2001.
Spencer, William. *Germany Then and Now.* Danbury, Conn.: Franklin Watts, 1994.
Yancey, Diane. *The Reunification of Germany.* San Diego, Calif.: Lucent, 1994.

Travel Information
www.lonelyplanet.com/destinations/europe/germany/
www.travelforkids.com/Funtodo/Germany/germany.htm

History and Geography
www.infoplease.com/ipa/A0107568.html
www.bartleby.com/65/ge/Germany.html
www.cybergerman.addr.com/land.html

Culture and Festivals
www.germany-info.org/relaunch/culture/life/G_Kids/index.htm
www.learn-german-online.net/learning-german-resouces/public-festivals-in-germany.htm
www.germanculture.com.ua

Economic and Political Information
www.cia.gov/cia/publications/factbook/index.html www.germany-info.org
www.wikipedia.org

EU Information
europa.eu.int/

Publisher's note:
The Web sites listed on this page were active at the time of publication. The publisher is not responsible for Web sites that have changed their addresses or discontinued operation since the date of publication. The publisher will review and update the Web-site list upon each reprint.

For More Information

German Information Center
4645 Reservoir Road NW
Washington, DC 20007-1998
Tel.: 202-471-5532
Fax: 202-471-5526

German Embassy
4645 Reservoir Road NW
Washington, DC 20007-1998
Tel.: 202-298-4000

German National Tourist Office
122 East 42nd Street
New York, NY 10168-0072
Tel.: 212-661-7200
Toll-free: 800-651-7010
Fax: 212-661-7174

Embassy of the United States in Berlin
Neustädtische Kirchstr. 4-5
10117 Berlin
Federal Republic of Germany

European Union
Delegation of the European Commission to the United States
2300 M Street, NW
Washington, DC 20037
Tel.: 202-862-9500
Fax: 202-429-1766

Glossary

abbeys: Monasteries or convents.

affluent: Wealthy.

autonomous: Able to act independently.

biomass: Energy from organic materials, such as wood or grass.

biosphere: The region of the earth, including the surface and atmosphere, in which living organisms can exist.

blocs: United groups of countries.

capital: Wealth in the form of money or property.

capitalist: Of or relating to an economic system based on private ownership of goods.

Celts: An ancient Indo-European people who lived in central and western Europe in pre-Roman times.

chancellor: The head of government in a parliamentary democracy.

Cold War: A period of hostility between the Soviet Union and the West in which there was political conflict but no armed warfare.

compulsory: Required.

confederation: A group of allied states or countries.

conifers: Cone-bearing trees such as pines.

conservation: The preservation, management, and care of natural or cultural resources.

cosmopolitan: Having a worldwide scope.

deciduous: Any tree that loses its leaves in the fall.

deficit: In finance, when income spent exceeds income received.

deflationary: Undergoing or creating a lower level of economic activity.

eco-friendly: Done in a way that does not harm the environment.

entrepreneurial: Willing to take risks in order to make a profit.

excise: A tax on goods used domestically.

exploited: Taken advantage of.

feudal system: A medieval system in which vassals worked land from lords in exchange for military service.

fiscal: Relating to financial matters.

fords: Shallow parts of a river or stream where people, animals, and vehicles can cross.

frescoes: Paintings done on a wall or ceiling by brushing watercolors onto damp plaster.

geothermal: Relating to the heat produced in the Earth's interior.

gross domestic product: The total value of all the goods and services produced within a country in a year.

guest workers: Temporary immigrants allowed into a country to fill specific jobs without being granted the privileges of citizenship.

information technology: Computer sciences.

infrastructure: The public systems, services, and utilities that are necessary for economic activity.

integration: The act of combining parts or groups into a whole.

lignite: A type of brown, soft coal.

meander: To follow an indirect route, often one that has many twists and turns.

mediums: The methods an artist uses or categories in which an artist works.

metropolises: Large cities.

migratory: Moving from one region to another, often based on weather changes.

nationalism: Devotion to a nation.

nationalist: Someone or something that stands for the rights and interests of the nation.

nation-state: An independent state recognized by and able to interact with other states, especially one composed of people of one nationality.

navigable: Passable by ship or boat.

neutral: Unaffiliated, not taking sides.

nobility: The aristocratic class.

parliament: A legislative body made up of representatives.

picturesque: Something that is very attractive.

pivot: A small point around which something larger turns.

proximity: Nearness to.

quota: A maximum permitted number or quantity.

ratified: Officially approved.

recession: A decline in economic prosperity.

reneged: Failed or refused to fulfill a promise or obligation.

reparations: Compensation demanded from a defeated nation by a victor in a war.

scorched-earth policy: In World War II, the Soviet Union's tactic of destroying all crops, equipment, or other resources that could be useful to the advancing German army.

service sector: The part of the economy made up of businesses that provide service to others.

socialism: A political system in which the means of production and distribution are controlled by the people.

solidarity: The act of standing together, presenting a united front.

sovereignty: Governmental independence; freedom from outside control.

stagnancy: A state of inactivity in which no movement or development occurs.

stringent: Strictly controlled or enforced.

subsidies: Grants given by the government to support enterprises that benefit the public.

sustainable: Using natural resources without destroying the ecological balance of a particular area.

tariff: Tax levied by governments on goods, usually imports.

temperate: Without extremes.

unification: The act of bringing together.

virtuosos: Exceptionally talented performers.

INDEX

PICTURE CREDITS

BIOGRAPHIES

AUTHOR

Ida Walker is a graduate of the University of Northern Iowa and did graduate work in Museum Studies/Art History at Syracuse University. She enjoys studying the history and cultures of other countries.

SERIES CONSULTANT

Ambassador John Bruton served as Irish Prime Minister from 1994 until 1997. As prime minister, he helped turn Ireland's economy into one of the fastest-growing in the world. He was also involved in the Northern Ireland Peace Process, which led to the 1998 Good Friday Agreement. During his tenure as Ireland's prime minister, he also presided over the European Union presidency in 1996 and helped finalize the Stability and Growth Pact, which governs management of the euro. Before being named the European Commission Head of Delegation in the United States, he was a member of the convention that drafted the European Constitution, signed October 29, 2004.

The European Commission Delegation to the United States represents the interests of the European Union as a whole, much as ambassadors represent their countries' interests to the U.S. government. Matters coming under European Commission authority are negotiated between the commission and the U.S. administration.